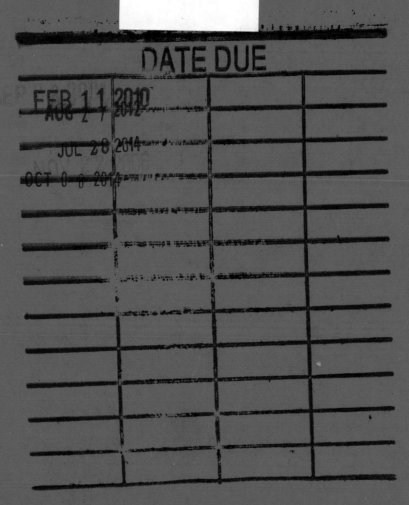

First Day, Hooray!

Nancy Poydar

Holiday House / New York

Library of Congress Cataloging-in-Publication Data
Poydar, Nancy.
        First day, hooray! / Nancy Poydar.—
        p. cm.
        Summary: All over town, Ivy Green and her bus driver and her
teacher and the other school employees get ready for the first day
of school.
ISBN 0-8234-1437-X
[1. First day of school—Fiction. 2. Schools—Fiction.]
I. Title.
PZ7.P8846Fi 1999
[E]—dc21   98-19312
CIP   AC

For my favorite teachers,
M. Virginia Biggy and Marion Gorham

It was almost fall, and all over town things were aflutter. Everyone was getting ready for tomorrow.

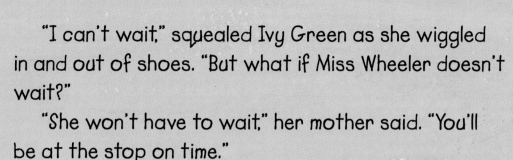

"I can't wait," squealed Ivy Green as she wiggled in and out of shoes. "But what if Miss Wheeler doesn't wait?"

"She won't have to wait," her mother said. "You'll be at the stop on time."

At the corner store, Ivy bought a lunchbox with stars.
"What if someone forgets lunch?"
"No one goes hungry," her mother said. "If someone forgets, you'll share."
Ivy bought raisins...to share.

At the brick building on the hill, Miss Wheeler went over her route. "Squirrel Hill, Rosemary Street...pick up Ivy Green. So many stops to learn!"

Mr. Handy buffed the hall. "Desks to lug...paper towels to load. So much still to do!"

Mr. Masters went over notes. "Colored paper...welcome signs. Will it all get done in time?"

Ms. Bell hung alphabet letters...wrote name tags. "Henry, Eric, Yasameen, Ivy..."

At her house, Ivy asked, "What if I can't find Ms. Bell's room?"

"Someone will show *you*," her mother answered.

"See my new shoes," Ivy said.
"I see," said her father. "I see! Calm down."

As the vacation sun cast its last long shadows, things finally did calm down. Ms. Bell turned off the lights.

Mr. Masters ate macaroni with his family.

Mr. Handy watched the news with Mrs. Handy.

Miss Wheeler soaked.

Ivy Green put on her pajamas.

"What'll you do when Miss Wheeler picks me up?"
Ivy asked.
"Wave and wave," her mother answered.

"And what'll you be
doing when I find Ms. Bell's room?"
"Imagining you with your friends," her father said.
Ivy imagined Ms. Bell's room.

At the brick building on the hill, Ms. Bell's room waited.
Shy moon shadows crisscrossed polished floors.

Name tags covered the table by the door: Christy, Ryan, Tyrone, Tom, Ned, Jody, Leah...Ivy.

Ivy was fast asleep.
All over town it was bedtime.

Ms. Bell pulled
on her nightgown.

Mr. Masters flossed.

Mr. Handy set the clock.

Miss Wheeler snored. "Snorkle, snurgle...snort."

Then, as sure as autumn leaves fly, wild
dreams drifted and billowed.
Ivy's hurry-scurry dream. Miss Wheeler's
missed-a-stop dream.

Ivy's no-lunch dream. Mr. Handy's not-mopped-in-time dream.

Ms. Bell's names-gone dream.
Mr. Masters's pajamas-on dream.

Ivy's which-door dream.

But with the wink of dawn...

...even the wildest dreams are gone.

Now the sun beams through the trees. It shines on Ms. Bell's alphabet letters, wakes up Mr. Masters's baby, glitters in Mr. Handy's coffee, makes Miss Wheeler's cat restless, and floods Ivy's bedroom when her mother snaps up the shade. "It's time!"

Time to get dressed.
Be at the stop.

Time for Miss
Wheeler to drive.

Time for Mr. Handy to unlock doors.

Time for Mr. Masters to greet.
Time for Ms. Bell to say,
"Good morning, Ivy Green."

And it's time for Ivy to hear stories, share crackers, and feed fish.

Time for Ivy to stack blocks, paint pictures, and write her name. "I.V.Y."

Why?

Because it's the first day. Hooray! The waiting's done. Ivy's school has finally begun.